Tiger and Mouse
The Gift of Helping Others

by Theodore Allen Lightfoot
Illustrated by Elizabeth and Phillip Armstrong

Help someone else and don't ask for anything in return. What you get will be bigger than what you gave.
--Author's translation of Luke 6:35

For Laura
- T.A.L

Quote by Kahlil Gibran: "You give but little when you give of your possessions. It is when you give of yourself that you truly give."
- P.A & E.A.

© 2012 Theodore Allen Lightfoot
Illustrations © 2012 Phillip and Elizabeth Armstrong
Edited by Julia H. Young
ISBN-10: 1470016605
ISBN-13: 978-1470016609
LightfootBooks@gmail.com

One bright morning a tiger cub named Tiger trotted into the jungle. He saw a tiny mouse whose name was Mouse. Tiger asked him, "Where are you headed?"

"To the field," said Mouse.

"Oh boy!" Tiger said, and jumped around. "I want to come with you and play, play, play!"

Mouse barely stopped to answer. "You can come along," he said, "but I won't have time to play. I'll be much too busy."

Tiger bounced, following Mouse into a warm, green field.

Mouse got right to work. He sniffed around. He looked on top of stumps. He looked under leaves. He **finally** found a tiny, delicious nut. Then, he couldn't believe his luck. He lifted a leaf and found a red berry. He rolled them both to a tall, yellow flower.

Tiger played, played, *played!*

He leaped through the grass, shouted, and plopped down in front of a berry bush that was speckled with juicy, red berries. But he didn't pick any. He jumped up and chased a butterfly around the field.

Mouse searched and searched and sniffed and sniffed. He looked up, he looked down. But he only found one more little, tiny, baby berry. He went back to the yellow flower. He tried to pick up his yummy treasures. He tried to pick them all up and walk home. He could not. He did not have enough paws.

He picked up one little nut and headed home.

Mouse rushed and rushed toward his home. He almost ran into Tiger.

Tiger saw that Mouse barely had any food. He said, "Hi Mouse. Is that little nut all you found?"

"This is all I could carry," Mouse replied.

Tiger saw the red berries by the yellow flower. He said, "Maybe you can come back and get those berries later."

"Yes, maybe," Mouse squeaked.

Tiger followed Mouse onto the sun-speckled trail.

Mouse's tummy rumbled at the smell of the delicious nut. But he could not eat it yet. He had to carry it very carefully. He could not drop it. He could not bite into it.

Suddenly Mouse disappeared into a tree stump. Tiger looked inside to see where Mouse had gone.

Tiger saw Mouse. He also saw Mouse's mother and brothers and sisters.

Mother Mouse said, "Honey, did you find anything to eat?"

"Oh yes, Mother," said Mouse.

Mother Mouse carefully took the nut from Mouse and broke it into teeny tiny little baby pieces. She started to hand them out to all six teeny tiny little mice. "One, two…three, four…five and six."

Mother Mouse said, "Now, let's say grace." Each brother and sister had a part to say:

This yummy meal smells so great...
But while I'm emptying my plate...
Help me never to forget...
To slow down a little bit...
And thank you for a special love...
That flows around us and above...

"That flows around us and above," all the mice said together.

Crunch crunch, munch munch. In a flash, all the little mice ate every speck of their food. Tiger watched. The smallest mouse of them all, Mouse's baby sister, squeaked and said, "Mother, do I get any seconds today?"

"I'm afraid not, dear," Mother Mouse whispered. One by one, each mouse left the table and began to play, even though their tummies were still hungry.

Tiger felt a tear in his eye. He felt like rocks were jumbling around in his tummy. He felt like there was an apple stuck in his throat.

All of a sudden, he pointed his nose toward the field again.

His feet started galloping through the jungle. Then his legs were running toward the field, faster and faster.

Tiger burst into the field like wind through the trees. He jumped through the grass to the berry bush. He stood on his back legs and swatted at the bush's red berries.

Then, Tiger saw a tree with a million nuts hanging off its branches. He ran, jumped, and crashed right into it. If he tried, he could hit the tree hard enough to make the nuts fall down to the ground.

It hurt, but he crashed into the tree again and again. Soon, piles of nuts lay all around him.

Tiger hurt all over. He rammed the tree many times. But he got up and found a leaf and wrapped up all the nuts. He limped to the berry bush and gathered lots and lots of juicy, red berries.

But, he was not done yet. He ran to the yellow flower. He picked up the two berries that Mouse had left behind.

He grabbed the leaf that was now full of yummy mouse goodies and ran back into the jungle.

Soon Tiger was back at Mouse's home with a bigger pile of fresh food than the mouse family had ever seen.

Tiger opened the leaf outside Mouse's door. Nuts and berries rolled all over the ground. He disappeared into the jungle.

Mouse was playing with his brothers and sisters inside his home. Then, he smelled something very, very good.

"What is that delicious smell?" Mouse asked his Mother.

"What is that yummy, delicious smell?" Mouse asked his baby sister.

"What is that yummy, delicious, amazing, superb, delectable, wondersuperyumalicious smell!?!" Mouse asked all his brothers and sisters.

He peered through the door of his little mouse home. Slowly, he crept out into the sunlight.

Mouse's brothers and sisters and Mother saw the huge, glowing smile on Mouse's face. Carefully, they followed him outside.

Mouse and his family saw the super-huge pile of wondersuperyumalicious food.

They jumped. They giggled. They smiled. And they drooled. Mouse's baby sister jumped into the pile of food!

They couldn't believe their eyes. Each little mouse grabbed a nut and berry in each paw and opened their mouths.

But Mother Mouse stopped them. "Now children," Mother Mouse said, "Isn't there something we're forgetting to do?"

As Tiger walked away, he could hear tiny voices:

This yummy meal smells so great...
But while I'm emptying my plate...
Help me never to forget...
To slow down a little bit...
And thank you for a special love...
That flows around us and above...

"That flows around us and above," said Tiger.

Talk About it

Discuss with your child some activities you could do together to help people in need. Here are some ideas:

-Practice singing a couple songs and perform at a local retirement home.

-As a family, sponsor a child in another country through a reputable organization. Have your child write letters to the sponsored child.

-Have your child pick out canned goods around the house or at the grocery store to donate to a local food bank.

-Help an elderly neighbor clean up leaves in the fall, shovel snow in the winter, clean out the garage in the spring, or pick weeds in the summer.

-Be creative. The possibilities are endless!

Find the eBook for this title and part 2 of this series - Tiger and Mouse: The Pebble of Perseverance - at Amazon.com.

Visit the author and illustrators at TheoLightfoot.com ArmstrongArtDesign.com